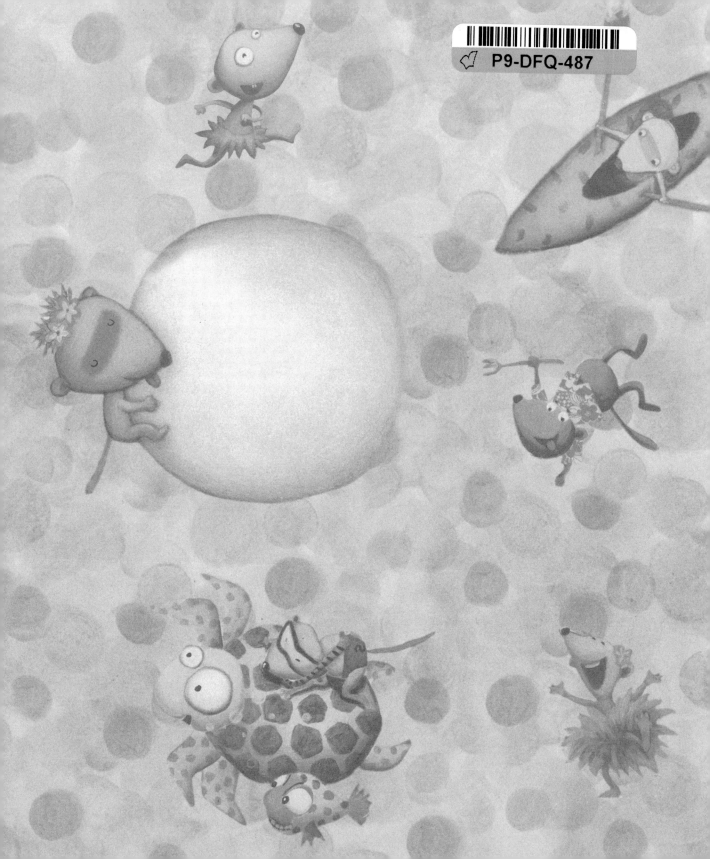

ISLAND HERITAGE™
PUBLISHING
A DIVISION OF THE MADDEN CORPORATION

94-411 Kō'aki Street, Waipahu, Hawai'i 96797
Orders: (800) 468-2800
Information: (808) 564-8800
Fax: (808) 564-8877
islandheritage.com

ISBN NO. 0-93154-865-9
First Edition, Second Printing — 2005

Mongoose, Mongoose, Stop! Don't Run

ISLAND HERITAGE™
PUBLISHING

Written by Antoinette Costello
Illustrated by Ariel Pang

Feeling sad, nothing to do.
I couldn't find anywhere to play.
Then suddenly a little mongoose
darted across my way.

2

I yelled,

"Mongoose, Mongoose,
Stop! Don't run.
I just want to have some fun."

3

He turned around and waved at me
as he climbed to the top of the coconut tree.

I shouted,
"Mongoose, Mongoose,
Stop! Don't run.
I just want to have some fun."

4

I would follow him
wherever he goes,
over the petroglyphs
in the old lava flows.

I cried,
"Mongoose, Mongoose,
Stop! Don't run.
I just want to have some fun."

DANGER
KEEP OUT

7

I chased him for what seemed like hours, through the plumeria and hibiscus flowers.

He must have been hungry. Boy, oh boy! He ran straight to a lūʻau and jumped into the poi.

I roared,
"Mongoose, Mongoose,
Stop! Don't run.
I just want to have some fun."

9

I called to him
but he didn't answer.
He was having fun
as a hula dancer.

I chuckled,
"Mongoose, Mongoose,
Stop! Don't run.
I just want to have some fun."

In the ocean I saw a dolphin spin.
Suddenly that crazy mongoose
grabbed its fin.

I begged,
"Mongoose, Mongoose,
Stop! Don't run.
I just want to have some fun."

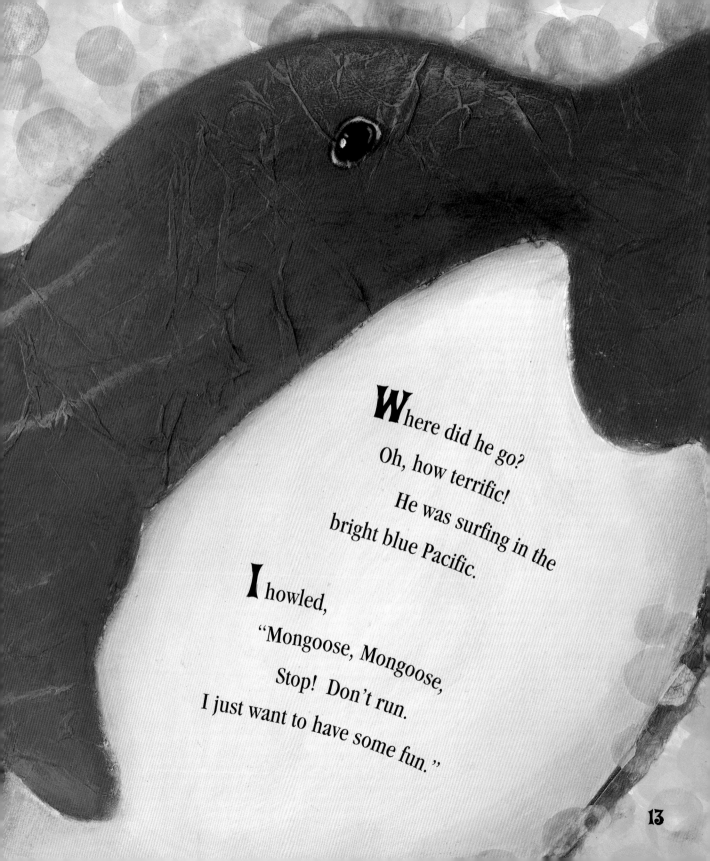

Where did he go?
Oh, how terrific!
He was surfing in the
bright blue Pacific.

I howled,

"Mongoose, Mongoose,
Stop! Don't run.
I just want to have some fun."

13

500 FT

10,000 FT

He grabbed a snorkel
to take a swim.
Then a green sea turtle
soon joined him.

I wailed,
"Mongoose, Mongoose,
Stop! Don't run.
I just want to have some fun."

Where was he now?
I couldn't figure.
Soon I spied him
riding in a fast outrigger.

I chanted,
"Mongoose, Mongoose,
Stop! Don't run.
I just want to have some fun."

16

I knew I would find him
sooner or later.
He was toasting a marshmallow
at a volcano crater.

I bellowed,
"Mongoose, Mongoose,
Stop! Don't run.
I just want to have some fun."

He could be anywhere,
but I'd take a bet
he'd be next to a waterfall
getting all wet.

I boomed,
"Mongoose, Mongoose,
Stop! Don't run.
I just want to have some fun."

Mongoose, Mongoose, I am done.
I just want to have some fun,
but all you do is
run, run, run.

20

I chased you all over the island,
from steep volcano to ocean sand.
I even saw you in the ocean deep,
but now I am going to get some sleep.

21

The mongoose turned and thought,
"Oh no!
Where oh where did you go?"
Looking around,
he started to giggle,

"Little child, little child,
Stop! Don't run.
I just want to have
some fun."

22

23

Glossary

coconut   the fruit of the coconut palm; its outer husk is peeled off to reveal a thick edible nut with coconut milk inside

crater   a large hole in the earth that forms a mouth of a volcano

hibiscus   the state flower of Hawai'i

hula   the native dance of Hawai'i

lū'au   a feast used to celebrate a variety of important events

outrigger   a canoe-like boat with timber rigged out from its side to prevent it from toppling

petroglyph   a carving or inscription on a rock

plumeria   a fragrant flower that grows in the islands

poi   a paste-like Hawaiian food made from taro root

surfing   the sport of riding in toward shore on the